KENNY ROGERS

presents

The Toy Shoppe

written by Kenny Rogers and Kelly Junkermann

song lyrics by Kenny Rogers, Steve Glassmeyer and Warren Hartman

*Look for the pages marked with a 🎵 for your chance
to sing along with Kenny and the Toy Shoppe gang!*

See the back cover for your Toy Shoppe companion audio cd.

Published by Addax Publishing Group Inc.

For Information address:
Addax Publishing Group Inc.
8643 Hauser Drive, Suite 235, Lenexa, KS 66215

Jerry Hirt
Art Direction/Design/Illustration

Sharon Snodgrass / Matt Fulks
Managing Editors

Thank you to Jim Mazza and Dreamcatcher Entertainment.
Special thanks to Brian Hakan and Associates, Paul Zamek and Becky French.

ISBN: 1-886110-94-8

Printed and Bound in Canada

1 3 5 7 9 10 8 6 4 2

ATTENTION SCHOOLS AND BUSINESSES
Addax Publishing Group Inc. books are available at quantity discounts with bulk purchase for education, business, or sales promotional use.
For information, please write to:
Special Sales Department, Addax Publishing Group
8643 Hauser Drive, Suite 235, Lenexa, KS 66215

Library of Congress Cataloging-in-Publication Data

Rogers, Kenny.
Kenny Rogers presents the Toy Shoppe / by Kenny Rogers and Kelly Junkermann.
p. cm.
Summary: A Christmas miracle saves Hank's used toystore from being closed by a dour businessman.
ISBN 1-886110-94-8
[1. Toy stores—Fiction. 2. Toys—Fiction. 3. Christmas—Fiction.] I. Junkermann, Kelly, 1954- II. Title.

PZ7.R62567 Ke 2000

[E]—dc21   00-028900

The Toy Shoppe

written by Kenny Rogers and Kelly Junkermann

As the story begins...

 MERRY CHRISTMAS

Hank Longley, owner of Longley's Toy Shoppe, was sad and upset as he stood in the town square across from his store. He watched the snow swirl around the workers as they put up a new sign in front of his toy shop. It read, "Future Home of Baxter Burger #52." You see, the Toy Shoppe had been in Hank's family a long time. Albert Longley, Hank's grandfather, had opened its' doors almost 100 years ago.

Hank stood there watching as Mary Claire, a news reporter from Channel 7, asked him how he felt about the new sign. "These toys are my

friends and they have been around a long time.

I will miss telling their stories to the children. But I have a few more days until the shop will close, so maybe something good will happen,"

Hank answered.

...so maybe something good will happen"

Mary and Hank finished their interview. Hank was entering the toy shop, when the children from the bus stop came running up.

"Mr. Longley, I got a 97 on my math test!" shouted Rosemary. The children knew with a 95 or higher on a test Hank would let them choose the story.

"Will you tell us about that stuffed dog?" they asked.

"This is a great story," said Hank as he picked up the stuffed dog. "This is a story about a mother's love, a child's fear and very possibly the first stuffed animal ever made.

"A long time ago, when this country was just starting, people sailed on ships from all over the world to come here to live. One of those families was the O'Malley family. But there was a problem. Aiden, their young daughter, had brought her dog she loved with all her heart. She had slept with this dog all her life. The ship's captain told Aiden she couldn't take her dog along. The voyage would be too long and he was concerned there wouldn't be enough food. The dog would have to stay behind.

"After weeks of watching Aiden's sadness, Mrs. O'Malley had a great idea. She took a blanket the dog had slept on, shaped it like a puppy and stuffed it with old rags. She gave it to Aiden who hugged it and curled up with it. For the first time on the journey Aiden went to sleep without crying."

"How did you get him, Mr. Longley? Did you live back then?" asked Kurt.

Hank laughed, "No, I'm not that old. Gather around. I haven't told you the best part. Do you see this hole?" he asked. "Late one night there was a loud KABOOM! The ship was surrounded by pirates. Cannon balls and musket shots were every-where. Poor Aiden clutched her dog tight. Then all of a sudden a shot from a musket came through the wall, *swoooosh*, and hit the stuffed dog. If Aiden hadn't been hugging the dog, the shot would have hit her. This dog saved Aiden's life.

"She called him HERO"

"She named him the same name as the dog they had left behind. She called him Hero."

"But, How did you get him, Mr. Longley?" asked Kurt again.

"You see, Aiden was my great-great-grandmother. The story and this dog have been passed down from generation to generation," explained Hank.

"I wish I had a dog like Hero," said Rosemary. "All I had was a big yellow cat and she never saved my life. She wasn't a hero or anything."

"Rosemary, you don't have to save a life to be a hero," said Hank. "I'll bet your cat was with you when you were lonely, or made you smile when you were sad, didn't she?"

Rosemary smiled, " Yes, she did, every day."

"Well then she did all she could. That's what heroes do. We all need heroes and we all have them somewhere," concluded Hank.

HEROES

Heroes
We all need heroes
Someone to believe in
Someone who believes in you
That's why they're heroes

They don't try to be heroes
Doing everyday what
Everyday people won't do

They tell you smile when you are hurting
If you can laugh when you feel blue

If you can cry when you are happy
And then the world will cry with you

If you can trust when trust is broken
And forgive along the way
If you can care when no one's watching
Then a light will light your way

Heroes
We all need heroes

The children were playing in the store when an older man with a dark hat came in and whacked the door with his cane. It was Mr. Baxter complaining, "Why do you kids come in here anyway? Half this junk is older than the houses you live in!" The kids hid behind Hank.

"Merry Christmas, Mr. Baxter," said Rosemary.

"I hate Christmas! Christmas makes me cranky. Santa and all his goofy reindeer.... Christmas trees all lit up.... and those Christmas cookies baking. I can't stand that smell," griped Mr. Baxter. He whacked his cane again, this time on the old jack-in-the-box. The kids went screaming out the door.

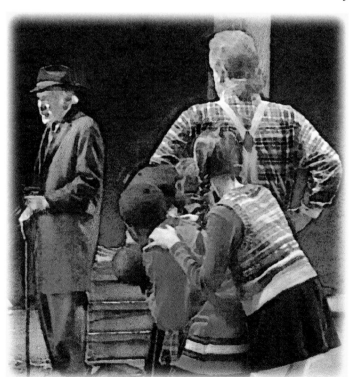

Mr. Baxter stared at Hank. "I don't like kids and I can't stand people who owe me money. I'm shutting you down Longley. Soon, this will be Baxter Burger number 52. I just dropped in to tell you that your toys will be moving to a new home...the garbage can!" Mr. Baxter's smile widened. "You can't stop progress and you don't know how happy that makes me. See you Christmas Eve, Longley," Mr. Baxter said as he left the shop.

"Merry Christmas to you too, Mr. Baxter," Hank muttered, hanging his head. He locked up his store and headed for home.

"Is he gone?"

Inside the Toy Shoppe, something magical was happening. The toys started to come to life.

Jack asked from inside his box, "Is he gone?"

"Is who gone?" wondered Bruno, a big overstuffed bear.

Cheeseball, a wise-cracking mouse answered, "Who do you think?"

"Bruno, we are talking about Hank," Foxy, a cute plush fox replied.

Riches, a rag doll, spoke up, "What are we going to do about Mr. Baxter? It's almost Christmas!"

"Sounds to me like we are all going to be homeless," Rags, his sister, cried.

"If we just had a plan," Riches said.

Just then, Rags had a great idea, "If we fix ourselves up, maybe someone would buy us and we could help save the Toy Shoppe."

"I think we would all make someone a great Christmas present!" Cheeseball exclaimed.

"That's it!" said Sarge, a large tin soldier. "Listen up toys we have a new mission. Think Christmas present!"

I WANNA BE A CHRISTMAS PRESENT

I wanna be a Christmas present
I wanna make someone smile
I want some child to wish for me

I wanna have lots of ribbons
I wanna be wrapped in style
I wanna be under the Christmas tree

I wanna be dreamed about for maybe
a month or two
I wanna go with a really big family
I'll go with you
Maybe there's a kid out there who's looking
for a toy that's not brand new
Well that's right up my alley
I'm looking for that kid too

I wanna feel the yuletide spirit
I wanna sing Christmas songs
I'm gonna be happy come what may

I wanna take a ride with Santa
I wanna be on his sleigh
I wanna be part of Christmas day
I wanna wake up with a lot of new friends
In a house where happiness never ends
I wanna be a Christmas toy someday

I wanna be a Christmas present
I wanna make someone smile
I want some child to wish for me

I wanna take a ride with Santa
I wanna be on his sleigh
I wanna be part of Christmas day
I wanna wake up with a lot of new friends
In a house where happiness never ends
I wanna be a Christmas toy someday

The next morning, Hank was working in the toy shop when in came Mr. Patterson. He had some important papers for Hank from Mr. Baxter.

"Mr. Baxter couldn't come today?" Hank asked, surprised that Mr. Baxter did not deliver the papers himself. He knew how much Mr. Baxter would have enjoyed telling him one more time how he was going to close the Toy Shoppe.

Mr. Patterson looked confused. "I guess you haven't heard," he answered. "Mr. Baxter had a serious accident and is in the hospital. Otherwise, I'm sure he would have been here. We're all hoping he'll be better for the big closing." He tipped his hat as he left the store.

"Mr. Longley"

The rest of the day was pretty quiet until the children were out of school. The bell above the door rang as all the children came running into the Toy Shoppe.

"Mr. Longley! Mr. Longley!" they shouted. "We have something for you."

"Whoa, slow down! What is it?" asked Hank. They were all excited. Becky climbed up on the workbench and plopped down a bag full of coins. "We wanted to help you save the store so we all cleaned out our piggy banks," Becky said.

"I smashed mine with a hammer," said Malik.

Becky held up the big bag of coins. "Together we have $42.83. This should help, shouldn't it?"

Hank was touched. "More than you'll ever know," he said. "In fact, if I save this store it's that $42.83 that's going to make the difference."

"My dad says you might not make it. He says it's like everything else. It's all about making money," said Percival.

Hank looked at the children. "Something good could still happen. Let's not give up hope just yet," said Hank.

MONEY ISN'T WHAT REALLY MATTERS

Money isn't what really matters
Fat cats just getting fatter
All the money in the world means nothing
Keep looking for only one thing
When you find it your heart will tell you
It's an impossibility to sell you
Nothin' in the world can buy you the wonders of

Love I know its love
For everyone this must be true
Love I'm sure it's love
And that is what I have with you

Money isn't a good or bad thing
Not enough can be a sad thing
Just remember the friends who love you
They really know the value of you

When everything is dark and scary
Or when you've got a lot to carry
That's when you can count your blessings from above

Love
Believe in love
For everyone this must be true
Love I'm sure it's love
Cause that is what I have with you

Money isn't what really matters
Fat cats just getting fatter
All the money in the world means nothing
Keep looking for only one thing
When you find it your heart will tell you
It's an impossibility to sell you
Nothin' in the world can buy you the wonders of

Love you know its love
For everyone this must be true
Love you know its love
Cause that is what I have with you

    "Can you tell us another story?" asked Rosemary. "That's what we're going to miss the most." She pointed up at a life-sized ballerina in a case. "You haven't told us about her yet. Does she have a good story?"

    "The best," replied Hank. "This is Giselle. You see, a long time ago the best clock makers in the world lived in Salzburg, Austria. The very best of them was Hans Klemmer. One day the people of Salzburg asked Hans to make a clock for the city. Well, Hans didn't want to just make any clock, so he locked himself in his shop and went to work. For six months he worked. Everyone could hardly wait to see his creation. Then one day the doors of the shop opened and there she was.... Giselle, the first life-sized animated toy ever built and the most beautiful ballerina the world had ever seen.

"People would come from miles around to watch Giselle dance each night as the big clock struck 8:00. The magical music box would play, a blue light would shine and Giselle would come to life. Giselle became a national treasure."

"What happened to her Mr. Longley? How did she get broken?" asked one of the children.

In a sad voice Hank said, "After a hundred years of flawless performances, she was suddenly struck by lightning and she never danced again. My grandfather heard they were taking her down so he bought her. She has been here ever since."

"Why would anyone want to buy her?" asked Gabby. "She was old, broken and couldn't even dance anymore."

Giselle became a national treasure.

Hank replied, "Because my grandfather believed toys were like people. Just because you're not perfect doesn't mean you aren't worth something. Giselle was so special that they never replaced her. Still, in the city of Salzburg, at 8:00 every night people come from miles around. The blue light shines and the magical music box plays. People stop and stare at the spot where Giselle danced. That is how special she is!"

Just then, Rosemary's mother came into the store to pick up the children. Hank walked them to the door and watched as they climbed into the van. The workmen were hammering away on the new Baxter Burger sign. Hank paused. "What's the use," he thought. After the van of children pulled away, he shouted out to the workmen, "Tell Baxter he wins. Tell him I quit!"

"Please don't do that, Mr. Longley. Please," said a small voice from behind him. Hank was a little embarrassed as he thought all the children had left for the day. He turned around and there stood a small girl.

"You can't quit, Mr. Longley. This is more than just a toy shop. You've got to at least hope something good will happen," she said.

"You can't quit Mr. Longley."

"I appreciate your words of encouragement, but there is a lot about business that you don't understand," said Hank.

"Oh I know that," she said. "But I also know that sometimes, if you hope with all your heart, good things will happen. Look around. This is such a special place, with all the older toys and all their stories. I've learned from you that each toy was made to make one certain person happy." She pointed up to a doll in a special case. "Like that one," she said.

Hank walked over and took the doll out of the case. One of its legs was missing.

"This was a gift given to my father. You see, as a young boy, Dad hurt his leg in a hunting accident.

"He was so sad that he stayed in his room day after day. Grandfather loved my dad so much that he asked what it would take to make him happy again. Dad said, a friend, someone who could understand his pain. So my grandfather, who was a master carver, carved him a friend… a wooden doll with only one leg. This doll became Dad's best friend and the toy he loved most. My grandfather wrote a poem on the back that changed my dad's life forever." Hank handed the doll to the little girl and she read the poem:

All are even in the eyes of God
Some get better starts
But it's those who have the least on earth
Who are closest to his heart."

She thought about it for a moment, then asked Hank, "Do you think it's true?"

"Yes," said Hank. "I do."

"May I borrow this doll?" she asked. "Just until Christmas? Before you say no, let me tell you it's for my grandfather."

Hank stopped her. "I have plenty of dolls here with both legs. Wouldn't that be better?"

"No, no," she persisted. "My grandfather has a bad leg, too. He got it trying to save me in an accident. This doll is perfect. In fact, he's Mr. Perfect. It'll be just what Grandfather needs to make him feel better."

Hank thought for a minute. "I don't know. This doll has never left the shop," he said.

"Mr. Longley, remember what I said about not giving up hope? For the past few days I've been hearing that my grandfather won't make it. But I don't believe it. I'm not giving up hope that something good will happen. I believe it will. Just until Christmas. I promise you'll get him back. Please?"

...if ever there is a time to trust, it's Christmas."

IF I ONLY HAD YOUR HEART

What do I do now

Look at my life and how it turned out

All of my caring, all of my dreams

So unimportant that's how it seems

It might have been different right from the start

If only I had your heart

Help me find a way

to finish this journey I started today

No one may know this deed that you do

It's simply a moment between me and you

These are the times that set you apart

If only you had the heart

I'll be there for you

Shoulder to shoulder

We'll make it through

The past is a dream I can't dream anymore

And the futures just doors never opened before

I'd take a deep breath and make a new start

If only I had your heart

"Mr. Perfect," Hank thought aloud. "Tell me, what's your name?" he asked.

"Katie," she answered.

"Katie, I'm going to trust you with this very special toy. Do you know why?" asked Hank.

"No sir," she said.

"Because it's Christmas and if ever there is a time to trust, it's Christmas," replied Hank.

"Thank you, Mr. Longley. I'll take special care of Mr. Perfect, I promise," Katie said as she began to leave.

"You know why I did it, Katie? I did it because you didn't ask for anything for yourself. You asked for someone else," said Hank.

She smiled, "But it is for me. Knowing my grandfather is going to be all right is the best Christmas present I could ever have."

"Merry Christmas, Katie," said Hank.

Katie's smile lit up the shop. "Oh it will, be Mr. Longley. It will be," she replied as she left.

What a day thought Hank as he looked back at the empty case that held the doll. He smiled as he locked the shop and headed for home.

Soon after Hank left, the toys began to wake up. They couldn't believe what had happened.

"Did you hear what she called him?" squeaked Cheeseball. "She called him Mr. Perfect."

"I never thought I'd see the day when Hank would give him away," said Sarge.

"A one-legged doll being called Mr. Perfect. I always knew there was something special about him," said Foxy.

"Well, I think we're all Mr. Perfect to someone," said Rags and Riches as they skipped across the floor.

"I'll miss him," said Bruno. "But did you see her smile? Tonight I'm going to dream about making someone that happy."

The toys all thought the same thing and went to sleep dreaming about making one child happy.

"Did you hear what she called him?"

The next day was Christmas Eve and Hank had to start packing up the toys. He flipped on the radio, hoping some Christmas music would cheer him up. Instead, there was a breaking news story.

"A patient woke up at the local hospital holding what appeared to be a toy. The hospital is calling it a miracle! More details as they become available," said the voice on the radio.

Hank went to get more boxes when a Baxter Burger commercial blared out. He quickly shut the radio off. Hank looked around the shop at Giselle, Bruno and Hero. With no hope left he said, "This is it guys. I want you to know something. I tried, I really tried."

The hospital is calling it a miracle!

I PROMISE YOU

I promise you whatever I do
You are the most important thing to me
I give my word I will be heard
No one will ever take you from me
And when you close your eyes
Know I will always come to you
And part of me will always be right there next to you

Someday there'll be just wait and see
Somewhere a place for you and me
Close your eyes
Know I will always come to you
And part of me will always be right there next to you

Someday there'll be just wait and see
Somewhere a place for you
Somewhere a place for you and me

Hank started to pack Hero in a box when the bell above the door rang. He could not believe what he saw. Mr. Baxter stood in the doorway. Hank was upset and threw the box down in disgust.

"Mr. Baxter! So your man Patterson was right. Only you would get out of a hospital bed on Christmas Eve just to make sure I got out!" shouted Hank.

"That's not exactly why I'm here," said Mr. Baxter.

Hank cut him off. "It doesn't really matter why you're here. I have some great memories from this old place and you can't take those away."

Mr. Baxter continued, "Longley, something happened to me yesterday and you must have had something to do with it." He held out Mr. Perfect. "It says here, *Return to Longley's Toy Shoppe,* so that's what I am doing. Maybe you can explain how I got it."

"That's not exactly why I'm here. "

"You're Katie's grandfather?"

Hank took the doll from Mr. Baxter. "I'm not sure," he said. "This little girl came by...she wanted to borrow....this doll just until Christmas." Hank stopped and looked at Baxter. "You're Katie's grandfather?"

Baxter leaned heavily on his cane and looked away so not to show his sadness. "I once had a granddaughter named Katie," he said.

Hank continued, "Katie wanted this doll. She named him Mr. Perfect because he was just like you."

Mr. Baxter looked up. "I would give everything I have if it could have been Katie. But my Katie died in an accident several years ago. It couldn't have been her."

Both men had trouble speaking.

"You know Longley," said Mr. Baxter breaking the silence, "I've always been a man who didn't believe in anything I couldn't see or touch or prove. I don't understand anything that's going on here. For years I've fought to get you out of here. Now you leave me no choice."

"It's over," thought Hank.

"Bring it on in kids!" shouted Mr. Baxter.

The front door burst open and the children wheeled in a large colorful sign.

Hank stood back and read it out loud, "Baxter and Longley's Toy Museum and Burger Joint." Hank was surprised and confused. "What does this mean, Mr. Baxter?"

"My burgers, your toys! I don't know why I didn't think of this before,"

Mr. Baxter stuck out his hand. "Partners?" he asked.

Hank grabbed his hand. "Sure, you bet," he answered.

A smile came across Mr. Baxter's face. "Merry Christmas, Hank."

"Oh, it will be, Mr. Baxter," said Hank. "It will be!"

THE TOY SHOPPE

If it's a miracle you're looking for
You'll find it right here in the Toy Shoppe
If you're looking for a place
You can find a happy face
It's the Toy Shoppe

And when you feel you need a friend
Who you know will be there 'till the end
In every day of every year
There is always someone here at the Toy Shoppe

So when you're lost and feel alone
You can find yourself a home
At the Toy Shoppe
In every heart there lies a child
Who has found a way to smile
At the Toy Shoppe

And if your world is closing in
There's a wonder waiting to begin
So when you're lost and feel alone
You can find yourself a home
In every heart there lies a child
Who has found a way to smile
So try a Christmas state of mind
And I promise you will find
There's a Toy Shoppe in your heart

THE END